WELCOME TO
PASSPORT TO READING
A beginning reader's ticket to a brand-new world!

Every book in this program is designed to build read-along and read-alone skills, level by level, through engaging and enriching stories. As the reader turns each page, he or she will become more confident with new vocabulary, sight words, and comprehension.

These PASSPORT TO READING levels will help you choose the perfect book for every reader.

READING TOGETHER
Read short words in simple sentence structures together to begin a reader's journey.

READING OUT LOUD
Encourage developing readers to sound out words in more complex stories with simple vocabulary.

READING INDEPENDENTLY
Newly independent readers gain confidence reading more complex sentences with higher word counts.

READY TO READ MORE
Readers prepare for chapter books with fewer illustrations and longer paragraphs.

This book features sight words from the educator-supported Dolch Sight Words List. This encourages the reader to recognize commonly used vocabulary words, increasing reading speed and fluency.

Enjoy the journey!

ABDOPUBLISHING.COM

Reinforced library bound edition published in 2018 by Spotlight, a division of ABDO, PO Box 398166, Minneapolis, Minnesota 55439. Spotlight produces high-quality reinforced library bound editions for schools and libraries. Published by agreement with Little, Brown and Company.

Printed in the United States of America, North Mankato, Minnesota.
092017
012018

THIS BOOK CONTAINS RECYCLED MATERIALS

Licensed By:

PUBLISHER'S CATALOGING IN PUBLICATION DATA

Names: London, Olivia, author. | Hasbro Studios, illustrator.
Title: Meet the ponies of Ponyville / writer, Olivia London ; art, Hasbro Studios.
Description: Reinforced library edition. | Minneapolis, Minnesota : Spotlight, 2018. |
    Series: My little pony leveled readers
Summary: Meet all of your favorite ponies in Ponyville, see where they live, and meet
    their pets.
Identifiers: LCCN 2017943446 | ISBN 9781532140938
Subjects: LCSH: Leveled reader--Juvenile fiction. | Ponies--Juvenile fiction. |
    Friendship--Juvenile fiction.
Classification: DDC [E]--dc23
LC record available at https://lccn.loc.gov/2017943446

Spotlight

A Division of ABDO
abdopublishing.com

MEET THE PONIES OF PONYVILLE

by Olivia London

LITTLE, BROWN AND COMPANY
New York Boston

ABDO
Spotlight

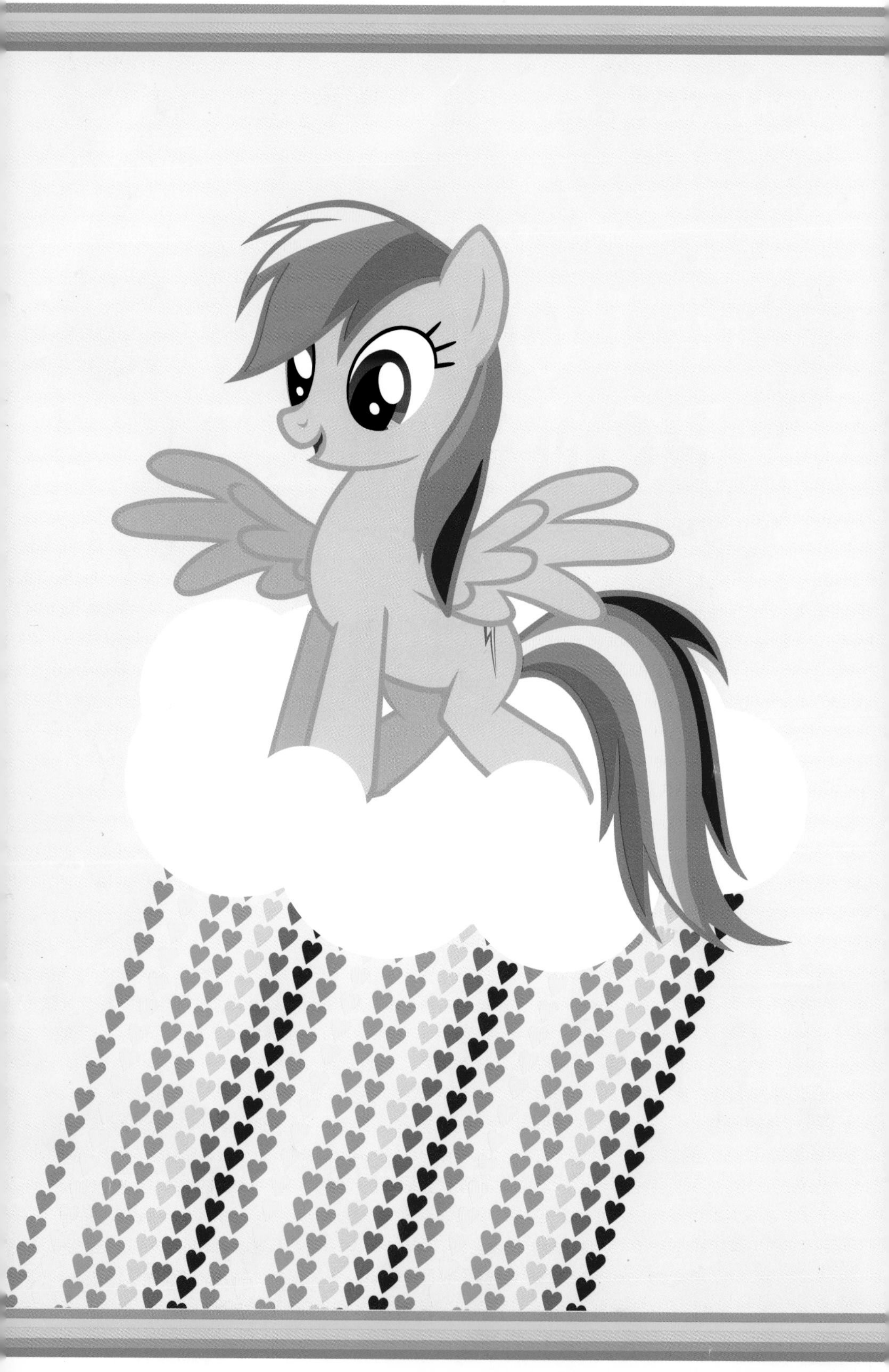

Attention, My Little Pony fans!
Look for these items when you read this book.
Can you spot them all?

unicorn

letter

orchard

dragon

In the center of Equestria
is the busy town of Ponyville.
Ponyville is a place
where all kinds of ponies
live together in peace.

Everypony who comes to visit
leaves with many new friends!
Let us meet the ponies of Ponyville
and learn why everypony loves them!

Twilight Sparkle is a unicorn.
She has strong magical powers,
stronger than most unicorns.

Twilight loves to learn new things.

Princess Celestia is her teacher.

She sent Twilight to Ponyville

to study friendship.

Each week, Twilight has homework.
She writes letters to the princess
about her lessons on friendship.
Twilight always makes sure
her homework is in on time!

Twilight has already learned
that everypony needs friends.
Now she has five best friends!

Spike is a baby dragon.
He lives in the library
with Twilight Sparkle.

He helps Twilight with everything!
Spike even helps her
find books to read for fun!

Spike also helps
Twilight with her homework.
He has a magical way of sending
Twilight's letters to the princess.

Spike loves eating stones that sparkle!
Oh, and he has a secret crush on Rarity.
Shhh!

Rarity is a unicorn.

She is a fashion designer.

She makes a dress for Twilight Sparkle.

Rarity uses her power to find
rare stones for the dress.
Twilight says,
"I do not like it—I love it!"

Rarity owns the Carousel Boutique.
That is where she sells her clothes.
She collects pretty things.
Her cat, Opal, does, too!

Rarity likes to give gifts.
She made everypony the perfect dress
for the Grand Galloping Gala.
Applejack's dress looks fancy!

Applejack loves apples!
She works in the orchard
at Sweet Apple Acres.
Her dog, Winona, helps on the farm!

The Apple family makes a lot
of yummy food at the farm.
Applejack often sells the food
at the Ponyville market.

Applejack works hard.

She always tells the truth.

Applejack cheers at the rodeo!

She likes to yell "Yee-haw!"

Applejack loves playing games,
but she prefers to win—
just like Rainbow Dash!

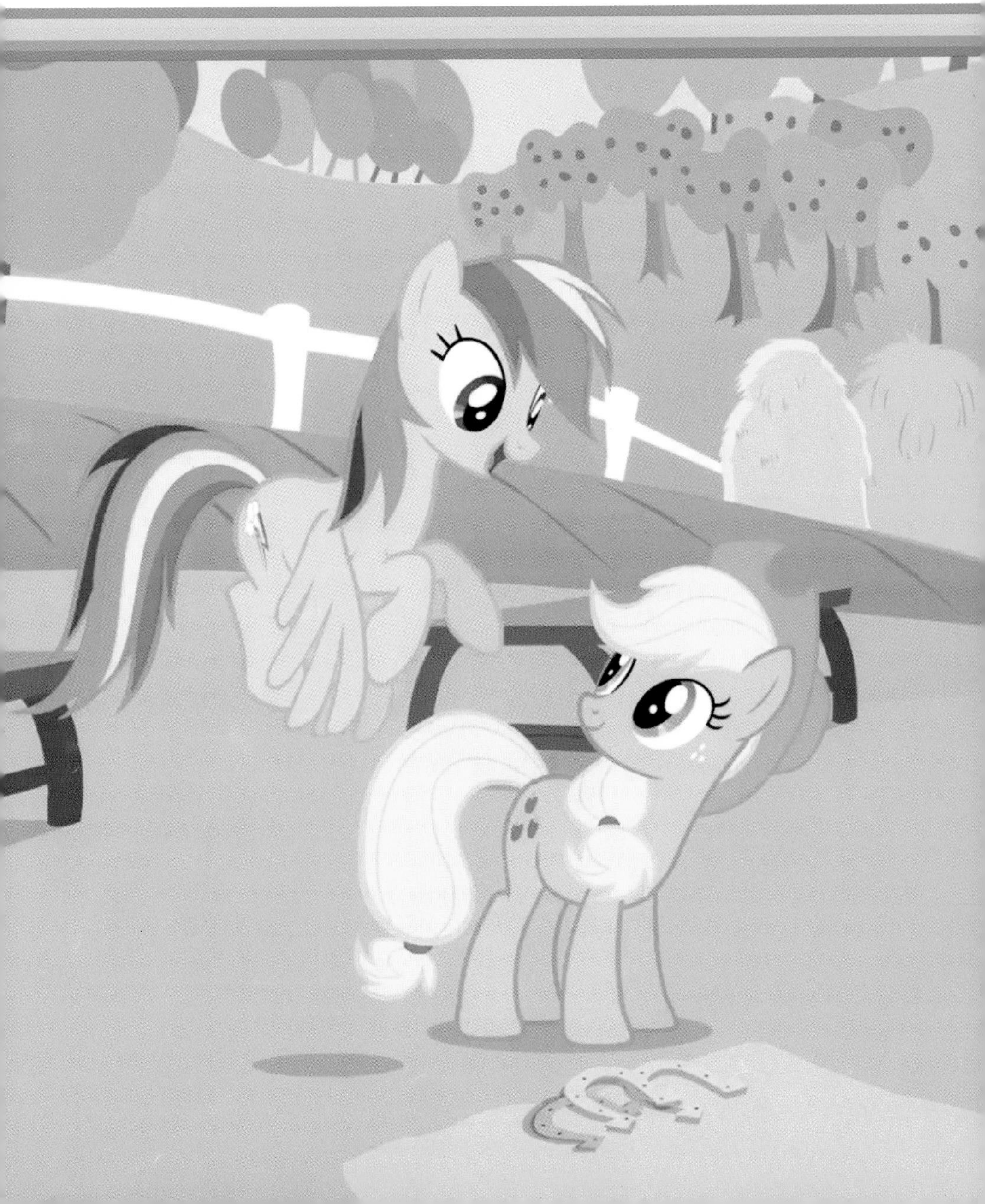

Rainbow Dash flies fast—
faster than anyone else!
She hopes to be on the
Wonderbolts flying team!

Rainbow Dash can fly so fast
that she can change the weather.

Rainbow Dash is a good friend.
But she also likes playing tricks
on other ponies!

She was born in Cloudsdale,
just like Fluttershy!

Fluttershy is graceful and kind.
She adores all animals.
Fluttershy lives near the forest
with her bunny, Angel.

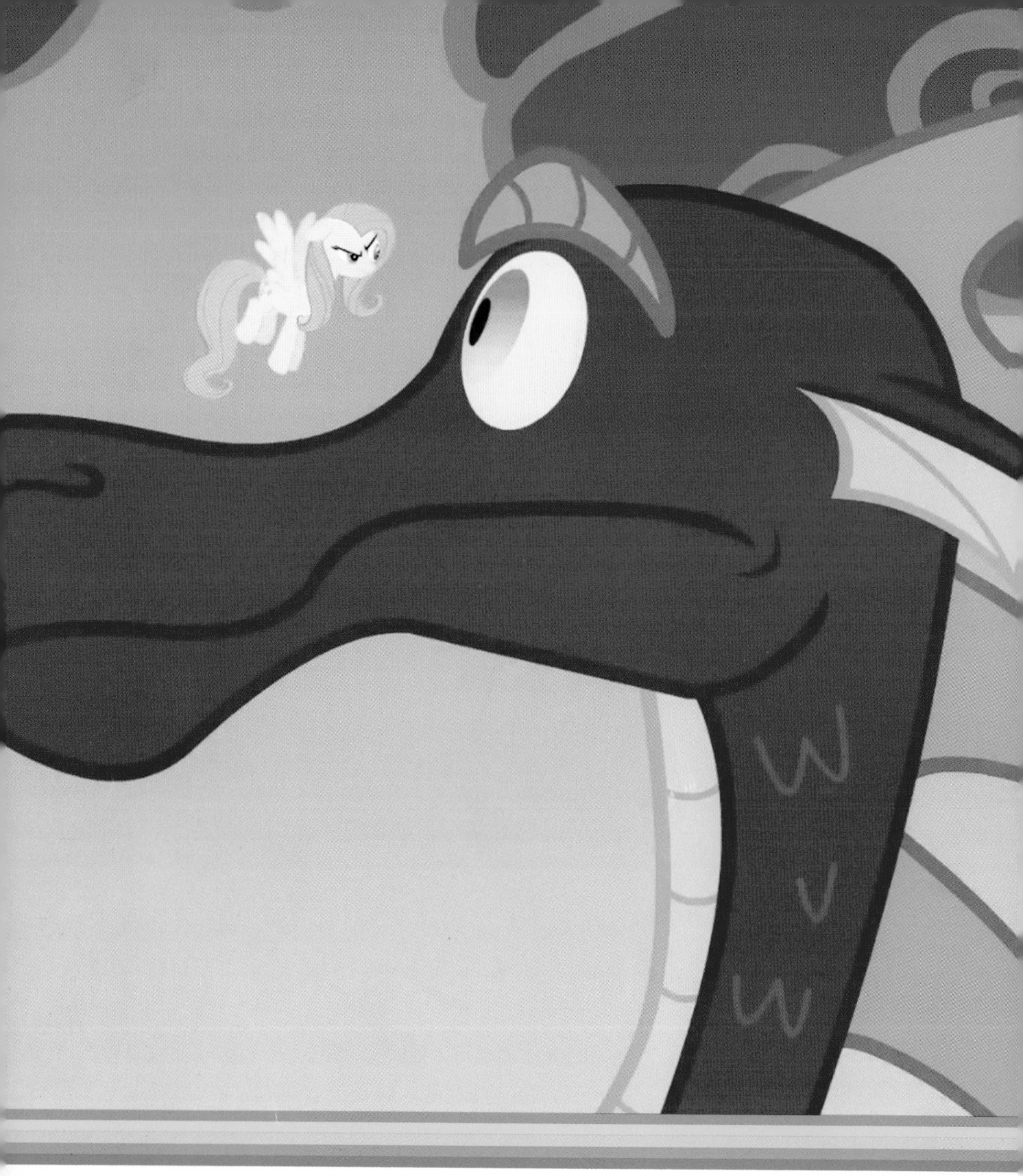

Fluttershy has a special skill
called the Stare.
It calms down wild animals—
even full-grown dragons!

She is shy around other ponies.
It is hard to hear Fluttershy
when she speaks.
She is not like Pinkie Pie!

Pinkie Pie has a lot of energy!
She loves to giggle and sing.
She bakes treats for the
SugarCube Corner bakery.

Pinkie Pie makes ponies smile.

She always says,

"You know what this calls for?

A party!"

Now you know what makes
the Ponyville ponies special.
Come back and visit them soon!

31901061082691